P9-DCM-074

THE Princess IN BLACK
and the HUNGRY BUNNY HORDE

THE *Princess* IN
BLACK
and the *HUNGRY BUNNY HORDE*

Shannon Hale & Dean Hale

illustrated by
LeUyen Pham

CANDLEWICK PRESS

This is a work of fiction. Names, characters, places, and incidents are either products of the authors' imagination or, if real, are used fictitiously.

Text copyright © 2016 by Shannon and Dean Hale
Illustrations copyright © 2016 by LeUyen Pham

All rights reserved. No part of this book may be reproduced, transmitted, or stored in an information retrieval system in any form or by any means, graphic, electronic, or mechanical, including photocopying, taping, and recording, without prior written permission from the publisher.

First edition 2016

Library of Congress Catalog Card Number 2015937113
ISBN 978-0-7636-6513-5

15 16 17 18 19 20 LEO 10 9 8 7 6 5 4 3 2 1

Printed in Heshan, Guangdong, China

This book was typeset in Kennerly.
The illustrations were done in watercolor and ink.

Candlewick Press
99 Dover Street
Somerville, Massachusetts 02144

visit us at www.candlewick.com

For Princess Ivy and Princess Cora,
who are more dangerous than they look
S. H. and D. H.

For Princess Ysee, Princess Madeleine,
and Princess Peyton
L. P.

Village

Goat
pasture

Chapter 1

Princess Magnolia and her unicorn, Frimplepants, rode toward the village. Princess Sneezewort had invited them to brunch. In anticipation, Frimplepants had skipped breakfast.

Brunch with Princess Sneezewort
meant soft rolls with butter.

Brunch with Princess Sneezewort
meant cheesy omelets. Brunch with
Princess Sneezewort meant heaping
platters of sugar-dusted doughnuts.

Frimplepants preferred brunch with Princess Sneezewort to anything in the world.

The café was so close now. The smell of hot bread rode the breeze. Frimplepants began to prance.

And then Princess Magnolia's glitter-stone ring rang. The monster alarm!

Frimplepants whimpered. He did not want to fight monsters right now. He wanted to eat doughnuts.

"No time to go back to the castle, Frimplepants," Princess Magnolia whispered. "To the secret cave!"

His tummy grumbled. Frimplepants hoped it would be a quick battle.

Princess Magnolia and
Frimplepants rode into
the secret cave. When
they came out the other
side, they were the Princess
in Black and her pony, Blacky.

Blacky reared up on his hind legs.
Look out, monsters! Never get between
a hungry pony and an especially good
brunch.

Chapter 2

The Princess in Black felt a pit in her stomach. Perhaps she was about to meet her greatest foe yet. Or perhaps she was just hungry. In anticipation of brunch, she had skipped breakfast.

Duff the goat boy was running toward them.

"Help!" he yelled. "There are hundreds of them! It's the worst monster invasion ever!"

"Fly, Blacky, fly!" said the Princess in Black.

Blacky did not fly. But he did run very fast.

They galloped into the goat pasture. The Princess in Black backflipped off the saddle. The Princess in Black raised her fists in Battle Pose.

But then the Princess in Black grinned.

Chapter 3

Duff the Goat Boy hurried back to the goat pasture. He liked to secretly study the Princess in Black's ninja moves. He needed more practice before he could become the Goat Avenger.

But when he caught up, the
Princess in Black was not battling
beasts. The Princess in Black was
making kissy faces.

That was not right. The Princess in Black fought the monsters that threatened his goats. Never had she petted the monsters. Never had she made kissy faces at them.

"Where are the monsters?" asked the Princess in Black.

Duff was out of breath from running. He pointed at the ground.

"Where?" asked the Princess in Black.

Duff pointed some more. There were a lot of bunnies to point at.

"I don't see anything besides these bunnies," she said.

"The bunnies . . . are . . . the monsters," said Duff.

The Princess in Black laughed. "Bunnies aren't monsters."

"But they came . . . from Monster Land," said Duff. "They hopped out of that hole. And they're eating my goats' grass!"

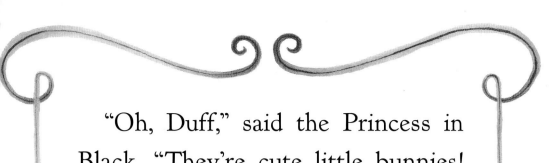

"Oh, Duff," said the Princess in Black. "They're cute little bunnies! What harm could they do?"

Chapter 4

Down in Monster Land, the bunnies had been bored. Bored and hungry.

With a hundred mouths, they had tasted everything. They had enjoyed monster fur. They had snacked on rock chips. They had dined on toe-nail clippings and lizard scales. And still they were hungry.

There was a hole in the ceiling of Monster Land. An interesting smell trickled down.

One brave bunny had poked its head through the hole.

Grass! An ocean of green grass!

"I must taste it," said the bunny.

The bunny munched some grass.

"This is yum," it said. "I should tell the others."

It told the others.

And soon, a horde of hungry bunnies had hopped up to the goat pasture.

Chapter 5

Blacky's stomach squeaked with hunger. Those bunnies sure seemed to relish the grass. Blacky wondered if it was especially delicious.

Blacky sniffed a deep green patch. It didn't smell like soft rolls with butter. It didn't smell like cheesy omelets or sugar-dusted doughnuts.

Blacky closed his eyes. He imagined the grass tasting as delicious as brunch. He opened his mouth wide and took a bite.

He sputtered and coughed. It hadn't tasted like doughnuts. It hadn't even tasted like grass.

Blacky's mouth was full of dirt. The bunnies had devoured the entire patch of grass.

And it looked like one was nibbling on the end of his tail.

Yes, one bunny was most definitely
nibbling on Blacky's tail.

Blacky swished his tail. The bunny
did not let go.

Blacky pranced about. The bunny
did not let go.

Blacky sat down. On his tail.

The bunny let go. The bunny
crawled away.

Chapter 6

Princess in Black, you have to stop these monsters!" said Duff.

He pulled at his hair. He paced this way and that.

"Are you sure they came from Monster Land?" she asked.

"Yes!" said Duff. "I saw them hop out of that hole."

"The poor things," said the Princess in Black. "They probably came here to escape the monsters. We must keep them safe."

Just then, a clawed paw reached out of the hole.

The first paw was followed by eight more. A massive, drooling, nine-pawed monster emerged.

It stood on its many hind legs. It opened its jaws.

It said, "ROAAARRRR!"

The bunnies stopped eating. They looked at the monster.

The monster started to say "ROAAARRRR!" again. But it only got as far as "ROAA—" It had noticed the bunnies.

The bunnies' noses wiggled.

The nine-pawed monster dived back into the hole.

The bunnies resumed eating.

"Did you see?" said Duff. "That massive, drooling, nine-pawed mon-ster was scared of the bunnies!"

"That's impossible," said the Princess in Black. "Bunnies aren't scary."

She petted the bunny on her lap. But instead of one bunny, now there were three.

"Um, are there more bunnies than before?"

Chapter 7

The pasture was no longer green. The bunnies had devoured nearly every blade of grass.

A few bunnies stuck like tree frogs to the big oak.

"Are they eating that tree?" asked Duff.

"Of course not," said the Princess in Black. "Bunnies don't eat trees."

More bunnies hopped onto the tree trunk. Others took to the branches. Seconds later, the tree was gone.

The bunnies smacked their lips.
"They ate the tree!" said Duff.
"They ate the entire tree!"

The Princess in Black didn't notice. She was petting the bunnies on her lap. Now there were six.

Bunnies began hopping onto goat backs. They nibbled goat hairs.

"They are eating my goats! They are eating my goats!" Duff yelled.

"But . . . but they're cute little bunnies?" said the Princess in Black.

A cute little bunny jumped onto a goat's head. It opened its tiny mouth wide. It clamped down on a goat horn. There was a sound like CHOMP.

The goat now had half a horn.
"AAH!" said Duff.

The Princess in Black looked down. A bunny was gnawing on her scepter.

Chapter 8

The Princess in Black stood up. Ten bunnies rolled off her lap. One was chewing a piece of her cape.

"You really are monsters, aren't you?" she said.

The bunnies wriggled their velvet noses. The bunnies waggled their fluffy tails. A tall one munched the bell off a goat's neck.

"Okay, monster bunnies, that is it!" said the Princess in Black. "You may not eat the goats. Go back in the hole."

The bunnies shuffled closer. One sniffed her shoe.

The Princess in Black pressed a switch on her scepter. It turned into a staff. She swung it at the bunnies.

SHIMMER SWEEP!

FEISTY FLASH!

The bunnies dodged her attacks. The bunnies blinked at her. The bunnies began to snack on a boulder.

"Duff, I don't know what to do," said the Princess in Black. "There are so many. And I can't even touch them."

"Try the Fearsome Flutter Clang," said Duff. "That scared away the big-eared monster last spring."

The Princess in Black extended her fan-shield. She hit it with her staff. A loud *CLANG!* echoed across the pasture.

The bunnies twitched their ears. They ate more rocks. They crowded around the goats. The goats bleated nervously. Especially the one who was missing half a horn.

"Back, bunnies! Back!" the Princess in Black shouted.

The bunnies didn't move. Except for the one taking dainty bites of her shoe.

Chapter 9

The bunnies watched the Princess in Black shout.

"The dark one sings for us," said one bunny.

The bunnies watched the Princess in Black swing her staff.

"It dances for us," said another bunny.

"We should ask it if it is food," said a bunny in the back.

"Are you food?" asked a bunny near her foot.

"If it wasn't food, it would tell us," said a bunny on a goat's head. "It would say, 'I'm not food.'"

"If it is food, we should eat it," said a bunny no one had noticed before.

"Perhaps it does not hear well," said the tiniest bunny. "Its ears are very small."

"Let us ask one more time," said the largest bunny. "All at once."

Hundreds of eyes looked at the Princess in Black. Hundreds of eyes blinked cutely at the same time.

"ARE YOU FOOD?" the bunnies were asking.

But the Princess in Black didn't hear any question. She just saw the bunnies blink cutely. She saw them sniff cutely and waggle their ears cutely.

"No answer," said a bunny in the middle. "It must be food."

Then all the bunnies said "EAT IT!" at the exact same time.

Chapter 10

The Princess in Black did not know the bunnies were speaking.
Duff did not know.
The goats did not know.

The hungry bunny horde spoke the language of Cuteness.

Cute sniffles. Cute waggles.

Cute hops. Only other cute animals could understand.

And that was why Blacky under-stood.

Because Blacky was not just Blacky the pony.

same ----------->

<------- same

same

He was also Frimplepants.
Frimplepants the unicorn.
And Frimplepants the unicorn was
as cute as they come.

Chapter 11

Blacky's tummy grumbled.

It growled. It roared. Blacky had a hard time thinking about anything besides brunch. The brunch he was missing.

Then he noticed the bunnies were saying something. About eating.

Did they want brunch? Were they wishing for rolls and omelets and doughnuts?

No. They were going to eat the Princess in Black!

The bunnies formed into one purple mass. Their mouths were open. Their teeth were shiny. Their black eyes stared at the Princess in Black.

Blacky leaped in front of his friend.

"Stop!" Blacky said with a soft neigh.

All the bunnies looked at Blacky.

"You may not eat her," Blacky said with a flutter of his eyelashes.

"It does not speak," the bunny with a mouthful of princess shoe told Blacky. "It is food."

"She is not yum," Blacky said with a frisky step. "She is yuck-tasting. All the good food is gone."

The bunnies looked around at the dry, dusty pasture.

"Surely there is good food in Monster Land," said Blacky.

"You have giant toenail clippings here?" asked a bunny off to the side.

"No," said Blacky.

"Scales? You have lizard scales to eat, maybe?" asked a bunny on Duff's shoulder.

"No scales," said Blacky.

"How about monster fur? You have to have monster fur," said a fat bunny leaning against a goat.

"None," said Blacky. "Don't toe-nails sound delicious? Yummy lizard scales. Tasty monster fur."

"I miss Monster Land," whimpered the smallest bunny.

"Me too," said hundreds of other bunnies.

"You should go back," said Blacky.

"YES!" said the monster bunnies.

They stampeded into the hole.

Chapter 12

Princess Sneezewort sat alone at a café table. There were soft rolls with butter. There were cheesy omelets. There were heaping platters of sugar-dusted doughnuts.

There was no Princess Magnolia. There was no Frimplepants. Even Princess Sneezewort's pet pig, Sir Hogswell, had wandered off.

The servers cleared the table. Brunch time was over.

Princess Sneezewort sighed. She relished Princess Magnolia's friendship. But often, Princess Magnolia showed up late. And often, her dress was on inside out.

"How very curious," Princess Sneezewort said to herself.

Where did Princess Magnolia go? And why did she dress in a hurry? Princess Sneezewort thought hard.

She had almost figured it out. . . .

But just then, someone shouted her name.

Was it Princess Magnolia with her dress inside out? No, it was the Princess in Black!

She was leading a herd of goats to the village pasture. The goat boy was telling everyone that the Princess in Black and Blacky had saved his goats. The crowd cheered.

"Princess Sneezewort!" she called. "Princess Magnolia sent me to apologize. She is very sorry she could not meet you for brunch."

"How very curious," said Princess Sneezewort. "Sadly, brunch time is over."

Blacky whimpered.

"Which means it's lunchtime," said Princess Sneezewort. "Will you join me?"

Blacky's eyes widened. His ears twitched. His tail swooshed. In the language of Cuteness, he was cheering, too.

"I'd prefer lunch with you to anything in the world," said the Princess in Black.

Frimplepants the unicorn didn't get brunch that day. But Blacky the pony lunched like a king.

SHANNON & DEAN HALE are the award-winning husband-and-wife writing team behind the Princess in Black books, illustrated by LeUyen Pham. Together they have also written the graphic novels *Rapunzel's Revenge* and *Calamity Jack*, both illustrated by Nathan Hale. Shannon Hale is the author of the Newbery Honor Book *Princess Academy*, the *New York Times* best-selling series *Ever After High*, and many others. About the Princess in Black, the authors say, "Sometimes our daughters wear princess dresses and play tea party, and sometimes they don capes and fight monsters. We wanted to write a character who does both, too!" Shannon and Dean Hale live in Salt Lake City, Utah, with their four young children.

LeUYEN PHAM is the illustrator of the Princess in Black books by Shannon and Dean Hale as well as many other books for children, including *God's Dream* by Archbishop Desmond Tutu and Douglas Carlton Abrams and *Aunt Mary's Rose* by Douglas Wood. About the Princess in Black series, she says, "I was never a very princessy girl, and I always preferred playing superheroes to playing girl games. I would have *loved* these books as a kid!" LeUyen Pham lives in California with her husband, who is also an artist, and her two young boys, who are superheroes by day and mini-monsters by night.